HOW TO PEE

POTTY-TRAINING FOR GIRLS

TODD SPECTOR, M.D.

Illustrated by
ARREE CHUNG

The Five Mile Press

I would like to dedicate this book to my children, Noa and Abe, who bring me happiness every day and inspire me to think like a kid. Thank you, Erica and Amy, for your hard work and diligence putting this book together with me—I would never have done it without you. Thank you, Daleet, for being a loving and supportive wife who reminds me every day what I am capable of. Finally, thank you to my patients from whom I have learned everything about medicine. —T. S.

For Peregryn and Juniper —A. C.

The Five Mile Press Pty Ltd
1 Centre Road, Scoresby
Victoria 3179, Australia
www.fivemile.com.au
Part of the Bonnier Publishing Group
www.bonnierpublishing.com
This edition published in 2016 by The Five Mile Press Pty Ltd
Copyright © 2016 text by Todd Spector, M.D.
Copyright © 2016 illustrations by Arree Chung

First published 2016 by
Henry Holt and Company, LLC
Publishers since 1866
175 Fifth Avenue
New York, New York 10010
mackids.com

Printed in China

5 4 3 2 1

GETTING STARTED

Many parents find potty-training frustrating, with false alarms and the inevitable accident. The truth is that all children, left to their own devices, will become potty-trained eventually, especially when they become physically aware of how uncomfortable a wet nappy is and, of course, when they realise that Mummy, Daddy, or a Big Brother or Sister use the potty!

When my wife and I started to potty-train our son, Abe, we invented a method called freestyle. Abe would make up styles for using the potty, and we would try to guess what they were. Instead of worrying about when he would be ready or how long the process would take, we decided to have fun with it. The result was a lesson and a game that kept the whole family laughing and inspired a book—*How to Pee: Potty-Training for Boys*.

Many of Abe's styles included props—masks, swords, light sabres, hats—and we encouraged him to be as wacky as possible. He liked to pee outside, so we designated a few areas where he could do this in our garden. Of course, we also found ways to bring the game inside to the toilet. Abe was quickly potty-trained, and even a year later, he would come up with a new style, using his creativity—and keeping our bathrooms clean.

This same method is just as fun and successful for girls. When our daughter, Noa, came along, we felt much better prepared and excited to share her older brother's method with her. We loved seeing how she made it her own, using magic wands, fairy wings, tiaras, and wigs as props.

I hope this book will spark your imagination (and keep you laughing) while you and your girl follow the simple steps to mastering the art of potty-training.

—Dr Todd

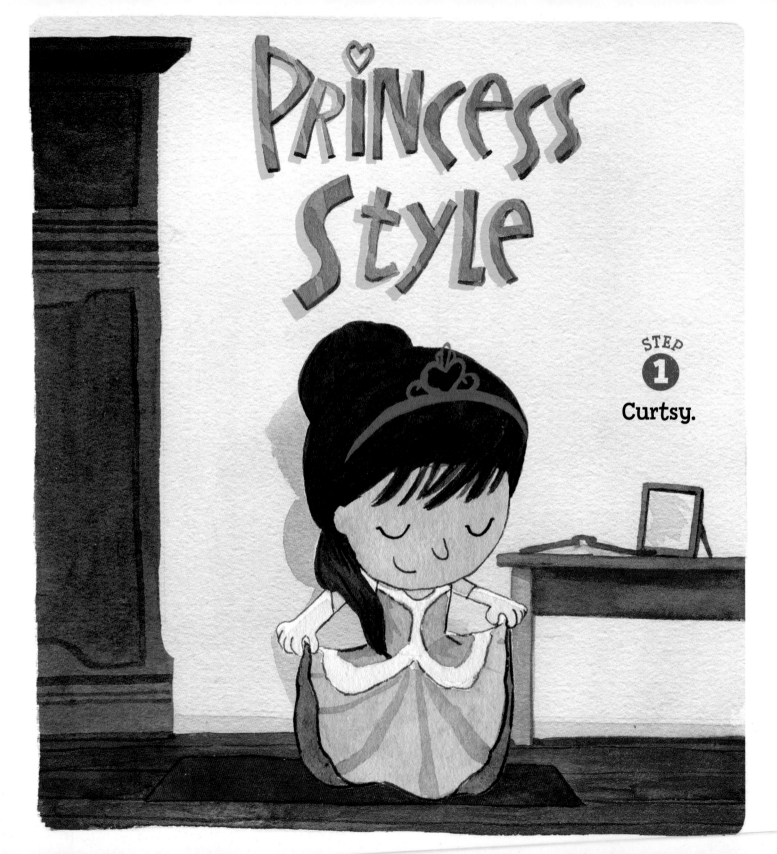

Princess Style

STEP 1

Curtsy.

STEP 2

Greet your people.

STEP 3

Kiss the prince.

STEP **4** Sit upon your throne.

Fresh Air Style

STEP 1

Stroll into the garden.

STEP
4

Water the plants.

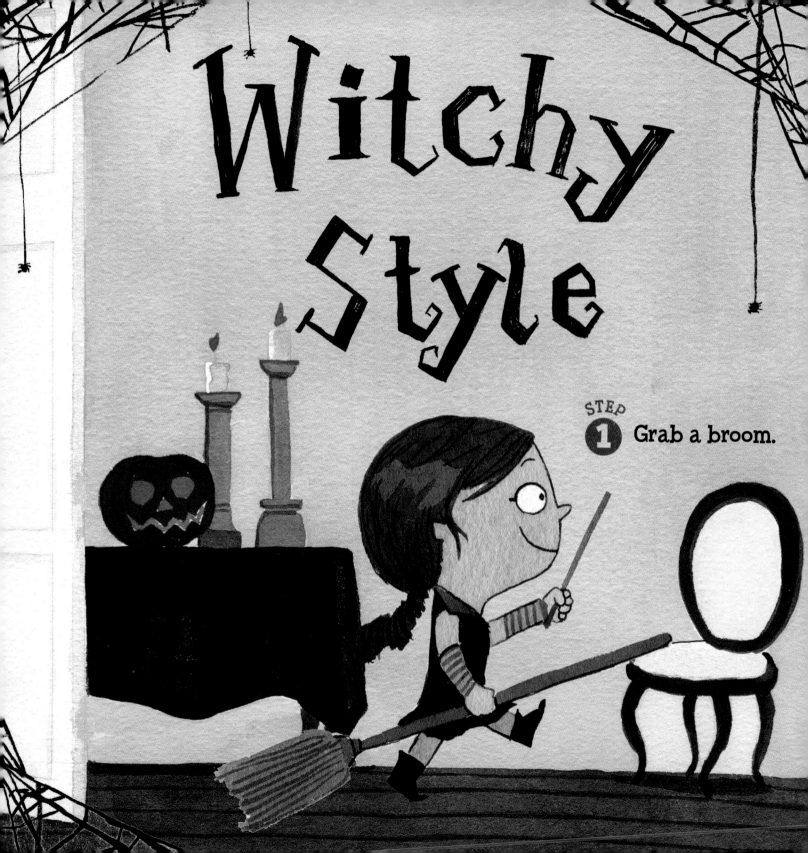

Witchy Style

STEP 1 Grab a broom.

STEP 2 Put on your pointy hat.

STEP 3

Raise your magic wand.

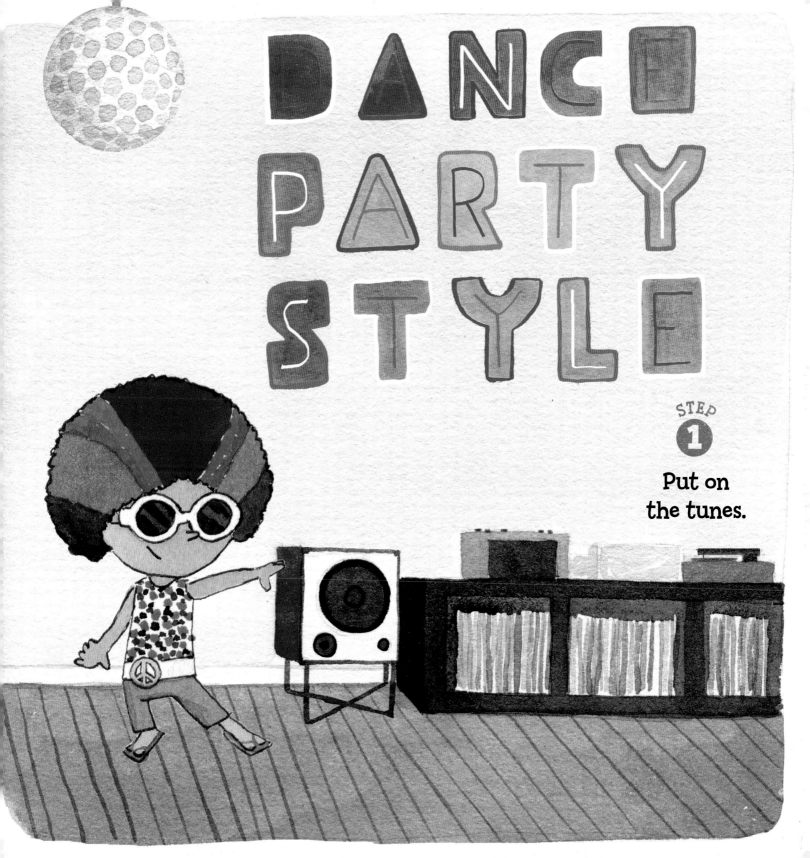

DANCE PARTY STYLE

STEP 1

Put on the tunes.

STEP
2

Turn on the
disco lights.

STEP 3

Wave your glow sticks.

STEP 4

Shake your booty and get down!

Tea Party Style

STEP **1**

Send the invitations.

You're Invited
to a party

Set out your finest china.

Pour the tea.

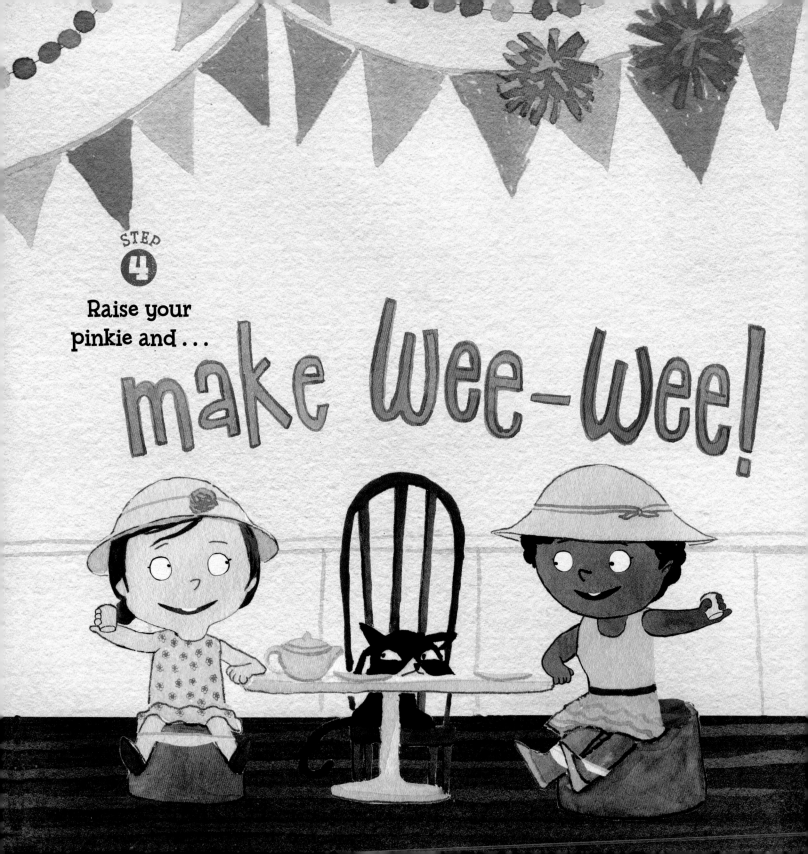

Royal Ball Style

STEP 1

Hang the streamers.

STEP 2 Find a fancy dress.

STEP 3 Don your feather boa.

STEP 4 Waltz your way to the toilet.

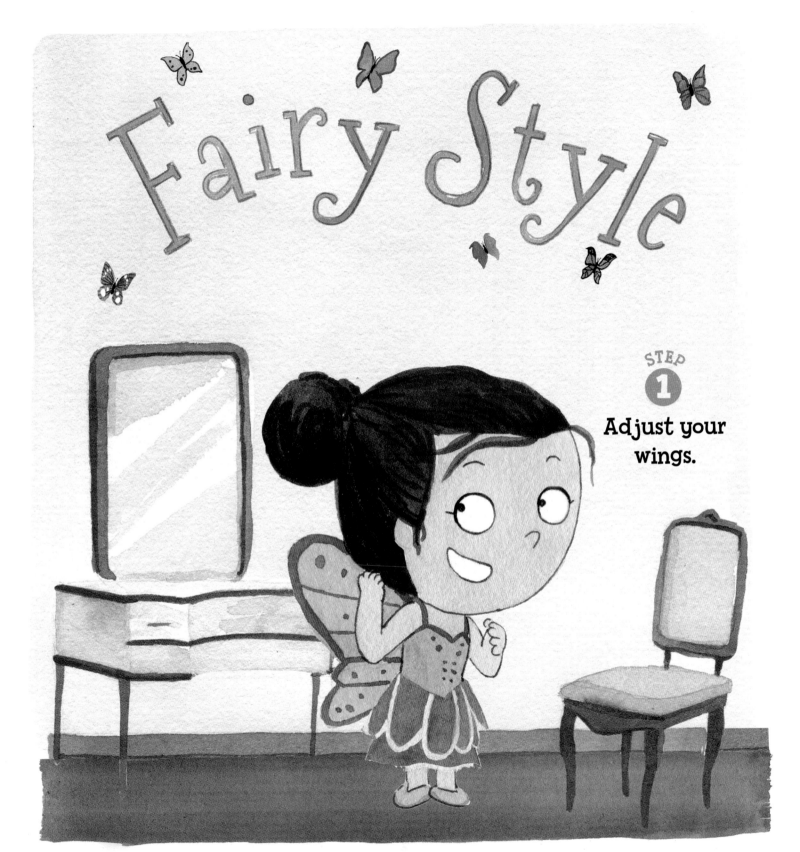

Fairy Style

Adjust your
wings.

STEP 2 Prepare for takeoff.

STEP 3 Fly to the bathroom.

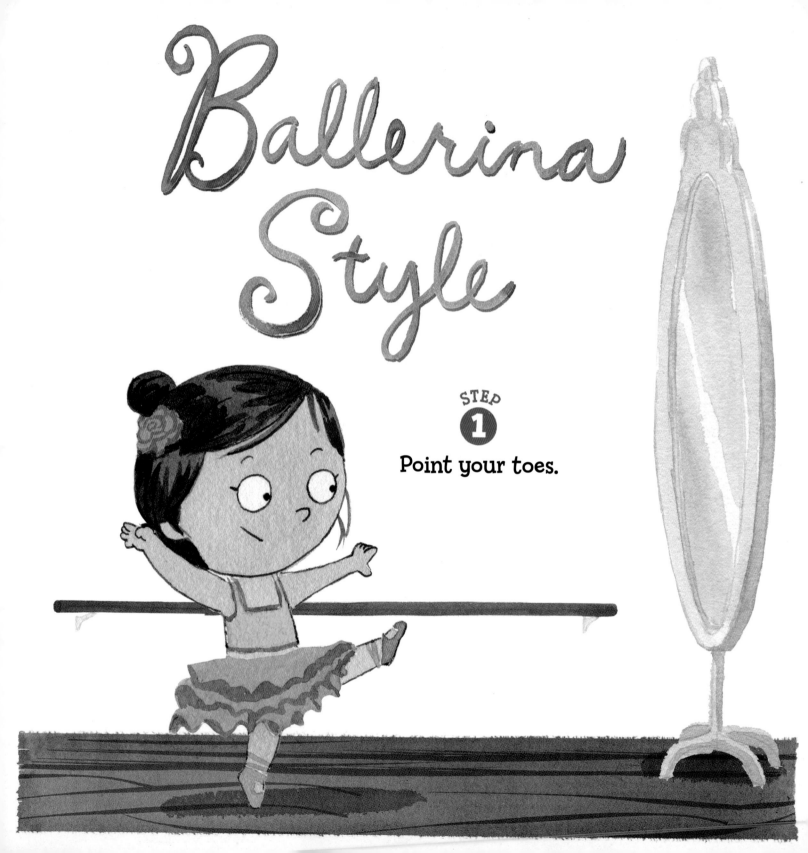

Ballerina Style

STEP

1

Point your toes.

STEP 2

Take tiny steps.

STEP 3

Twirl.

STEP 4

Bend your knees
over the potty.

LITTLE STAR STYLE

STEP
1

Watch the sky
turn to night.

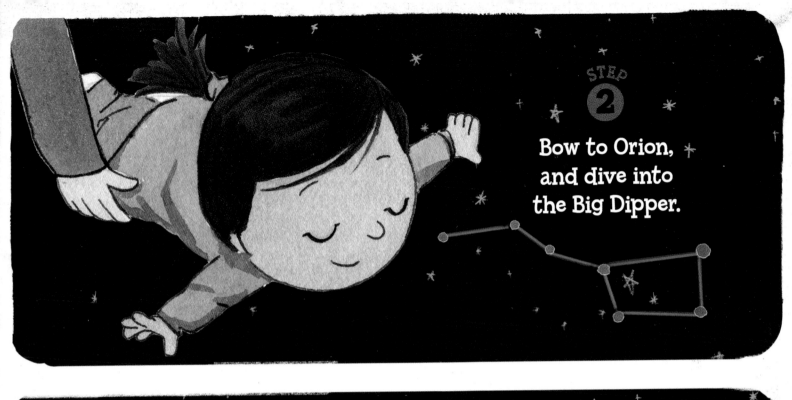

STEP 2

Bow to Orion, and dive into the Big Dipper.

STEP 3

Ride past the Milky Way.

TINKLE, TINKLE, LITTLE STAR...

GYMNAST STYLE

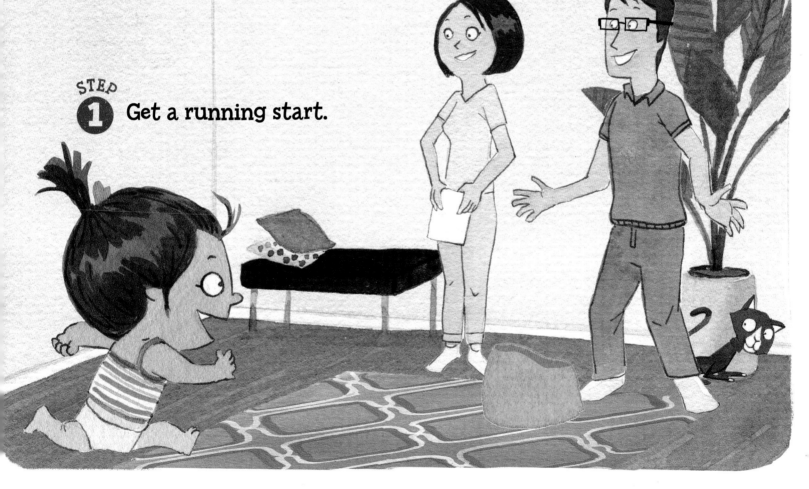

STEP 1 Get a running start.

STEP
2 Mount.

STEP
3
Release.

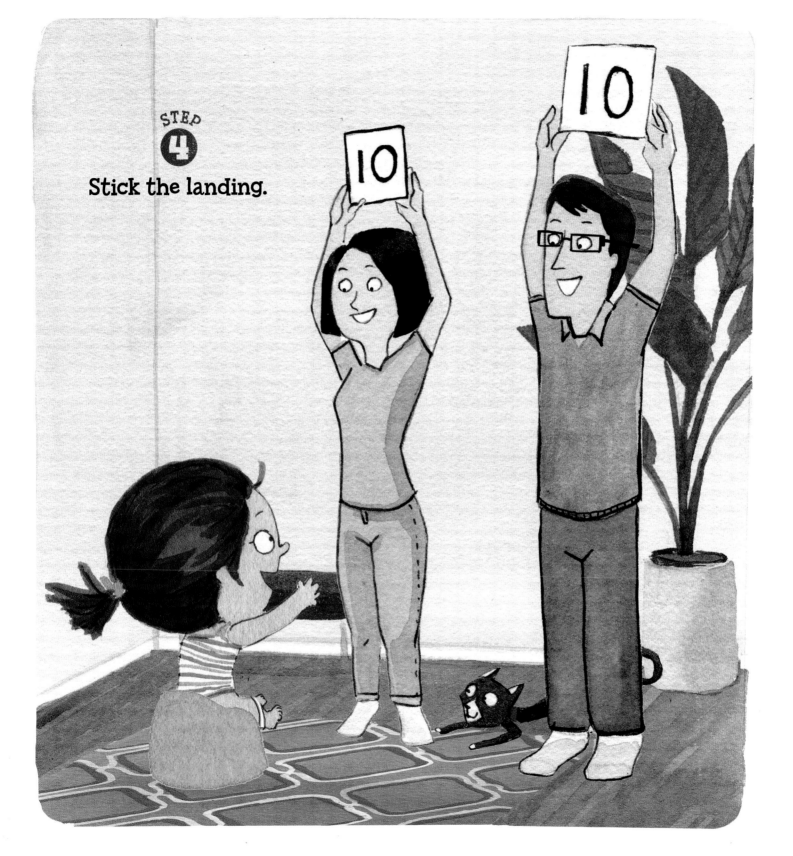

STEP
4

Stick the landing.

A NOTE TO PARENTS

As a Family Practice physician, I'm always looking for ways to explain to parents that being potty-trained is a normal developmental milestone. One of the first things I tell anxious parents is that I see a lot of kids who are not potty-trained at age three, but I almost never see four-year-olds in nappies. This usually helps parents relax and buys a little more time for the child to figure it out on her own. In addition, girls seem to be able to potty-train (control their sphincters) slightly earlier than boys do, so don't be surprised if your daughter wants to use the potty earlier than your son did.

Today, much of the pressure to potty-train early comes from preschools and day cares that insist children are out of nappies before they are admitted. But many two-year-olds are not developmentally ready to potty-train. That said, I believe that learning not to wet yourself is a very basic human instinct and children are aware of this as early as eighteen to thirty-six months old. Unfortunately, because modern nappies are so sturdy and comfortable, children are barely aware when they are wet, so they can't respond to the stimulus and learn how to stay clean. I'm not saying using nappies on your child will do her harm; it just might delay this milestone.

I often tell parents that when children start to ask for a new nappy or mention that they are peeing, they are ready to be potty-trained. A training potty should be your first investment. Buy a small, simple one and place it next to your toilet. Your child will see you using the potty and, as in other things, will model her behaviour on yours. At first, she may sit on the potty while still wearing a nappy. Do not worry: she is well on her way to figuring it out on her own.

Another tip I give parents is to get rid of the nappy. Let your child run around naked for a few hours at a time. Eventually, she will figure it out. There might be a few accidents, but soon enough, she'll remember what she's seen you do and make her way to the potty to do her business.

A FEW BASIC RULES

1. Don't pressure your child. Remember, this is a natural process.

2. Don't punish your child for having accidents.

3. Don't worry if your child is not potty-trained even if it seems as if all the other three-year-olds you know are.

4. Don't worry about a few accidents on your floor.

5. If your child says she has to pee and she isn't near a potty, don't rush her to the toilet. Let her hold it for a moment as you go calmly to the bathroom. If she has an accident, see rule 4.

6. If your child regresses and starts to have accidents again, it's okay to use a training nappy. It's best if you have your child put it on like underwear.

7. If your child continues to have accidents and it is causing stress for your family, see rule 1. Don't be afraid to go back to nappies for a while and try potty-training again in a few weeks. But make sure your daughter has a few hours a day without a nappy on to get used to the sensation.

GOOD LUCK!